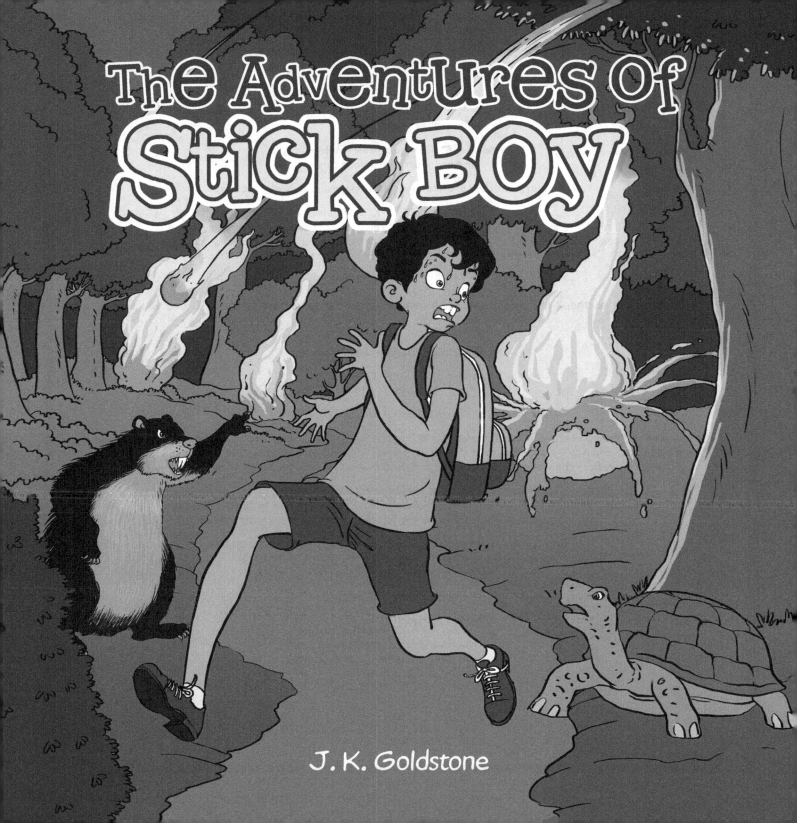

Order this book online at www.trafford.com
or email orders@trafford.com

Most Trafford titles are also available at major online book retailers.

I would like to thank my oldest son Isiah, who inspired me to write this book. I love you son!

Printed in the United States of America.

ISBN: 978-1-4907-3385-2 (sc)
978-1-4907-3384-5 (e)

Library of Congress Control Number: 2014907025

Our mission is to efficiently provide the world's finest, most comprehensive book publishing
service, enabling every author to experience success. To find out how to publish your book,
your way, and have it available worldwide, visit us online at www.trafford.com

Any people depicted in stock imagery provided by Thinkstock are models,
and such images are being used for illustrative purposes only.
Certain stock imagery © Thinkstock.

Trafford rev. 04/21/2014

Trafford PUBLISHING® www.trafford.com
North America & international
toll-free: 1 888 232 4444 (USA & Canada)
fax: 812 355 4082

It was the last day of school, and Zaak was dreading the summer. Summertime meant no kids, no gym, no homework, and no fun. It also meant more chores and more time with his mother and Grandpa Mootey. Zaak was an only child. His mother never let him do anything because he was twelve years old and only weighed seventy pounds. He was allergic to almost every airborne allergen, and he had already broken eight bones since birth. His mother was very protective of him and did not want him to get hurt in any way.

He was always the one picked on at school, but at least at school he was not by himself. The mere presence of other kids gave him the illusion that he belonged. Although it was the end of his first year in junior high and he still had made no friends, it was better than being at home alone with Grandpa Mootey.

Ring! Ring!

Well, there goes my summer, he thought while the bell rang. He sat at his desk, looking around at all the other kids, listening to them brag about all the exciting things they would be doing during the summer. "Matt? Are you getting up?" his teacher asked. "It's Zaak, Mr. Fowler," Zaak responded. "Oh, okay. Are you leaving? I have to lock up."

"Yes, sir," he said as he slowly stood up from his desk. He left the classroom, looking back as if he was leaving behind a prized possession. He walked down the hall as slowly as he could. As he walked toward the exit door, one of the kids tripped him. All the kids around laughed hysterically as Zaak slid across the floor into the door. Zaak got up, gathered himself, and walked toward the door. The kids were all still pointing and laughing at him while he walked out of the school. He felt a breeze on his backside, and he turned and noticed that he had split his pants when he fell. "Great!" he yelled.

Zaak's house was a few miles away from the school, using the road, but he always took a shortcut through the woods. He walked this way every day, but for some reason, this day was different. Usually there are squirrels chasing one another, deer prancing in the distance, or rabbits bouncing around here and there. However, there was no sign of anything. "Well, isn't that swell. Even the animals refuse to come around me. I am so sick of this. Every day it's the same thing. I wake up, I go to school, I am teased, I go home, and I do diddlely! Now I have to spend the whole summer being babysat by a big fat baldheaded old person!" he yelled angrily.

The woods were his home away from home. Anytime he was upset, he would go into the woods, watch the animals, and listen to the sounds of the forest. It always made him feel better. Zaak was almost home, when he sat down by the big magnolia tree that he used to sit under with his father, carving wooden artwork. Just then, a large group of animals came rushing toward him. He jumped up and ran for his life as he screamed at the top of his lungs. "Ahhhhhhh! Get back!

4

Stop! Holt! Be gone! Ahhhhhh!" He ran into the house and slammed the door behind him. Zaak reached into his pocket, pulled out his inhaler, and ran to the window to look out. Then he took a dose of his inhaler to catch his breath. When he looked, the animals were all running past into the woods at the back of the house. It seemed as if they were scared of something.

Zaak still had a few more hours before his mother was home. Usually he did his homework and made him something to eat, but he had no homework and he was too curious about the animals to eat. He was so curious that he left the safety of his house and went back out into the woods. When he got into the woods, he noticed a strange blue mist in the air. *What is this?* he wondered. The blue mist made him more curious about what was going on, so he went further into the forest.

He looked around to see what the animals could possibly have been running away from. Then he looked down and saw a small tree that was uprooted, lying on the ground. Strangely, the tree was shaped like a person. "Wow! This is so cool! I can make a stick man out of this!" he said happily. Seeing the man-shaped tree made him forget all about the strange blue mist. He grabbed the tree and dragged it all the way home and into his bedroom. Zaak had a fascination with wood because his father was an expert wood-carver, and he taught him everything he knew. He carefully examined the tree and discovered that it was mahogany. "This is perfect for carving," he said to himself. Then he went and grabbed his father's wood-carving materials and started on his masterpiece. As he was working, his mother came home. She walked into his room to check on him. To her surprise, she saw all the carving materials. "Are those?" She paused and started to tear up. Zaak nodded his head and stood up to give her a hug. As they hugged, his mother said, "You know you could have used the shop, right? It would have been a lot less messy."

"Not yet," Zaak answered.

"I understand. Well, at least these things are being put to use," she said. Then she kissed him on the top of his head and walked out of the room. Zaak or his mother had not even looked at his father's carving tools since his sudden death two years prior. "Oh, and by the way, Grandpa will be over tomorrow while I'm at work!" his mother yelled from the other room. Zaak took a deep breath, shook his head, and started back working on his project.

He used a carving knife to shape out the body parts. Then he drilled holes where the body parts connect and put wire through to hold them together. Then he used a single piece of wood shaped like a cylinder and stuck it in the top of the body to make a neck. Now there were only two things left. The stick man needed a name, and Zaak still had to make a head for it. "I will name you Limb since you came from a tree," he said proudly. Unfortunately, he didn't have a piece of wood that was the right shape to make the head. It was too late to venture back out into the woods, so he would have to wait until the next day to find it.

The next day when Zaak woke up, his grandfather was already there. Grandpa Mooty was a large tall man with a bald head and a beard that was all the way down to his chest. Zaak came out of his room, and he was greeted with a great, big bear hug. "Hey there, Zaak Attack! What's my only grandson been doing since I saw him last?" he asked as he dropped him from his arms. "Nothing much, Gramps," he replied. "Your mom told me you were in your room with your father's carving stuff. That's a good start, son. That's a good start."

"Thanks, Gramps."

"You wanna go down to the river and do some fishing with your old grandpappy after breakfast, kid?" "Maybe later, Gramps. I have to go take care of something right now." After meeting with his grandfather, Zaak rushed into his room, grabbed the stick man, and rushed out of the door and into the woods. He looked around for a piece of wood that was the right size to make a head, but he could not find one.

He searched for hours and hours, but still nothing. Finally, he gave up because it was getting late, so he headed back home. All of a sudden, the ground started to rumble and shake, blue mist filled the air, and the sky became dark and cloudy. He looked up and saw what seemed like snowflakes falling, but when one touched his skin, it burned him. "Ouch! This is fire ash!" he yelled dramatically. He was so far in the woods that if something happened, Grandpa Mooty wouldn't hear him. Zaak started to run as fast as he could through the woods, desperately trying to get home. Then he realized he dropped his stick man when he was burned by the ash. This creation was very important to him, so he ran back to get it. When he reached the stick man, ash was coming down like heavy snowfall. As the ash seared his skin, he picked up the stick man and started again to run. Then Zaak heard what sounded like a freight train coming toward him.

He looked around and saw nothing but ash falling. However, when he looked up, there where balls of fire the size of bowling balls raining from the sky. When the fireballs hit the ground, it sounded like bombs exploding. Suddenly, a fireball hit a tree right in front of him, and he fell and sprained his ankle. When he looked up, a huge golden fireball was falling from the sky, coming right toward him. Zaak tried to get up, but he couldn't stand. He realized there was nothing he could do to prevent the golden fireball from hitting him. Therefore, he held up the stick man to try to limit the severity of the impact. "Ahhhhhh!" Zaak screamed in fear. *Boom!* A gigantic earthquake shook the whole area of the woods where he was. There was smoke and fire everywhere. As the smoke cleared, Zaak lay there with his hands still out in front of him. "Oh my god! I'm alive! I'm alive!" he yelled as he danced around. "Wait a minute. I was just hit by a fireball. Why am I still alive? Where is Limb?" he questioned.

Then he realized that the fireball hit so hard that it made a crater in which he was at the bottom of. He looked around for a way to get out, but the crater was too deep. There was no way to get out. In desperation, Zaak jumped up to try to climb out and flew right out of the crater. Zaak couldn't believe it. He was actually flying! "This is awesome!" he shouted. He flew over the mountains and the river. He saw large fields with lots of crops. He even saw his house. "Oh no, Grandpa Mooty!" he said as he flew in for a landing. He tried to land and crashed into the barn. He dusted himself off and rushed toward the house. Just then, his mother ran out to see where the noise came from. "Ahhhhhh! Get away from me!" his mother screamed. Zaak tried to talk to her, but she ran into the house. He yelled for her as he stood there and banged on the door, but she locked it and wouldn't open it. "What's happening to me? First I'm flying, now my mom is afraid of me. What am I going to do now?" he expressed sadly.

Zaak decided to wait the night out in the woodshop. He went in and caught a glance at the mirror sitting on the floor in the corner. What he saw he could not believe. He looked again to make sure he wasn't imagining things. Somehow, he had been transformed into a stick man! "I look like Pinocchio! It's no wonder Mom was afraid of me! This can't be happening to me! I have to be dreaming! Please tell me I'm dreaming!" he screamed. Crying frantically, he started talking to his father. "Dad, if you're up there, I need your help. I don't know why this is happening to me. Maybe you can help me somehow. Please, Dad! I need you!" he cried loudly. Still crying, he made a cot and laid down. He cried himself to sleep, hoping that this was just a dream. In the middle of the night, Zaak's body doubled in size. When he woke up the next morning, he was in the middle of the woods. His feet were planted into the ground, and tree bark covered his whole body. "This is too weird. I guess it wasn't a dream after all," he said. He stepped out of the ground, and his feet looked like roots. When he saw this, he yelled loudly and ran until he was tired. When he stopped, he was by a river.

As he stood by the river, he cried. "Hello," said a kind voice. He looked around to see who it was, but he didn't see anyone. "Who's there?" he said as he sniffled. "Down here! It's me." called the voice. Zaak looked down, and there was a beaver that stood about three and one-half feet tall. "What's your name?" the beaver asked him.

"You can talk?"

"Umm, yeah."

"But you're a beaver."

"And you're a tree."

"That's funny!" Zaak said as he laughed loudly. "My name is Zaak."

"I'm Becky."

"How did this happen to you, Becky?" Zaak asked her. "Well, I was busy working on my house, when the ground started to shake, and these huge balls with fire on them started to fall down from the sky. The next thing I knew I was standing upright and talking," she said excitedly. Becky and Zaak became friends fast.

They talked about everything. Soon Zaak forgot all about his big dilemma. "Do you want to go swimming, Zaak?" Becky asked him. "Sure! I love to swim!" he told her. Becky and Zaak jumped in the river to swim. Becky swam down into the water, but when Zaak tried, he couldn't. The only thing that he could do was float. He couldn't go down because he was made of wood. Nevertheless, that didn't stop him from swimming. They swam all day long. They had so much fun that they lost track of time. Soon it began to rain, so they got out of the water. "We've got to get out of this rain!" Becky said. "Where do you live, Zaak?"

"Well, it's a long story. I—"

"No worries. You can sleep over at my house if you want."

"That's okay. I can sleep outside. I'm a tree, remember?"

"Oh, yeah. How could I forget?" Becky hurried into her home, and Zaak went to the edge of the forest and sat down. He began to think of his mother and father. "I really miss you guys," he said quietly.

The rain began to come down hard. Zaak thought of an umbrella. All of a sudden, out of his shoulders sprouted branches with flourishing leaves all over them. It kept the rain from falling on his head. "Wow! This is amazing!" he shouted. He was outside but no longer in the rain. Zaak planted his feet into the ground, got comfortable, and went to sleep.

The next morning while Zaak was still asleep, Becky decided to sniff him to see what type of wood he was. "Mahogany, I love mahogany!" she whispered to herself. "I shouldn't be doing this, he is my friend. But he smells so tasty! No Becky, stop this nonsense right now!" she whispered loudly to herself. But, the smell of his skin tempted her so much that she took a tiny bite of his arm. Becky's teeth clashing with Zaak's powerful wooden skin created a bright, blinding light. The bite didn't hurt Zaak because he was protected by his bark, but the light woke him. "What's going on?" Zaak asked as he yawned. Becky was still overwhelmed by the taste of his bark. As she came about, she seemed different. Her teeth were as sharp as razors, her tail was moving as fast as hummingbirds' wings, and her eyes were rolling about in every direction.

"Becky, are you okay? Zaak asked. "Wood! More! More!" she responded. Becky was no longer the sweet beaver he met by the river. She was now evil! She lunged at Zaak with her razor-sharp teeth and claws, but Zaak jumped out of the way and ran as fast as he could. "You can run, but you can't hide, Stick Boy! I know what you smell like!" she said with and evil voice. Zaak ran deep into the woods. He didn't look back even once. He wondered what Becky would do if she found him. He knew that she would never give up looking for him. *I must focus and see if I have any abilities that will protect me against the Becky the Beaver.* He thought to himself. As he walked through the forest, he became tired. He felt like he hadn't eaten in days. He saw a huge rock in the distance, so he went over and sat down. "Hey! What's the big idea? Do you know how heavy you are?" shouted a voice. It sounded to Zaak like Grandpa Mooty's voice. "Gramps, is that you?" Zaak said. He thought he must really be going crazy to think Grandpa Mooty would be out here. Suddenly, Zaak felt his body being lifted into the air. The rock was moving!

Zaak looked down, saw four legs and a long stretchy neck, and knew immediately that it was a turtle. This was the biggest turtle he had ever seen. "Are you lost?" asked the huge turtle. "I am very hungry, and I have nothing to eat," Zaak said sadly. The turtle, being wise, said, "A guy like you can find food anywhere as long as there is soil. You just plant your feet into the ground and *DIG IN! Get it? DIG . . . IN?*" Zaak jumped down and put his feet into the ground. A few seconds later, he felt as good as new. "By the way, what's your name, kid?"

"Zaak."

"Well, my name is Sheldon. It's very nice to meet you, Zaak."

Meanwhile, back at the river, Becky was asking questions of her own. She couldn't understand why, since the very moment she bit Zaak, she wanted him so bad. She had many foods to eat, being that she was a beaver and she was in the woods. She didn't even crave all the beautiful, tasty trees in the forest.

All she could think about was how good Zaak would taste cooked over a warm fire and glazed with honey. "I gotta have that kid!" she yelled. Becky became especially mad just thinking about having Zaak for dinner. She shrieked loudly, and with one swipe of her claws, she cut down a tree. Then she climbed to the very top of another tree and used her razor-sharp teeth to grind it to bits from top to bottom. Then she took her tail and fanned it so fast that the wind created a mini tornado, and she threw it at a nearby cottage. *Crash!* "I hope no one was in there!" She laughed. After that, she set off to find Zaak.

Zaak felt refreshed after putting his feet into the ground. He was ready to try to see what other abilities he possibly had. He told Sheldon about the Becky issue, and Sheldon had an idea. "We have got to get you ready just in case that crazy beaver comes back!" he expressed. Sheldon told Zaak to stick his feet in the ground and relax. Then Sheldon heard a noise. He looked around, but nothing was there. When he turned back to talk to Zaak, he was nowhere to be found.

"Hey, kid! Where'd you go?" yelled Sheldon. "I'm right here," Zaak said as he giggled. Zaak had camouflaged himself to blend into the trees, and Sheldon didn't know which one he was. "Okay, kid. That's enough. You can come out now!" Sheldon commanded. Just then, a root came up out of the ground and picked him up. "Whoa! Hey, what's the big idea? Put me down!" Sheldon said as he laughed. Zaak put him down and said, "Did you see that, Sheldon? That was so cool!" Although Zaak was excited about his newly discovered power, Sheldon told him that they had a lot of work to do. "Just a simple camouflage might fool me, but Becky knows wood. Not only that, but she knows what you smell like. She'd sniff you out of a lineup of one hundred trees," Sheldon told him.

Sheldon decided to take Zaak to the water to see if the water helps him as the soil did. Therefore, they went to the river. He told Zaak to try to drink some of the water and see what happens. Zaak took a small sip of the tasty river water. All of a sudden, he began to grow bigger.

Zaak was so fascinated that he drank more water. The more water he drank, the more he grew. He drank so much water that soon he was taller than every tree in the forest. Then he started to feel faint and weak. He stumbled around, and then he splashed into the river. Because of all the water he drank, he wouldn't float. Sheldon tried to pull him out, but he was too heavy. Then his body began to shrink. He got smaller and smaller, and all his bark disappeared. "Help! I'm drowning!" he cried. Sheldon pulled him out of the water and onto the beach. "Too much water is not good for any plant. You have to be careful not to drink too much," Sheldon advised.

Becky went through the forest, terrorizing animals and cutting down trees. "I'll find you if it's the last thing I do!" she screeched. Becky made wooden cages and put the animals in them. "I'll will capture all these idiot creatures and make them my slaves!" Becky hollered. Becky had really gone mad. The animals were all terrified. Becky told them, "Stop whining, or else I'm gonna grind you all up and make stew!"

"Excuse me, Your Queenliness. May I be of assistance?" something with a raspy voice interrupted. "Eww! Boy, you stink! What do you want?" Becky said with her nose covered. "I want to assist you in your endeavors to find this Zaak fellow you're searching for. I am Buteo. But you can call me whatever you want, my queen," he said as he bowed. Buteo was a large buzzard, with huge wings and long claws. "First, move away so I can breathe. Then tell me why I need your help." Buteo moved back a couple of feet and said, "I can fly over the top of the trees and look down to see if I can find him from an aerial view. That way we—I mean, you have a better chance at finding him."

"You're stinky, but you're smart."

"Just tell me what he looks like, Your Highness." At that, Becky pulled a tree up out of the ground and yelled, "Like this!"

"Well, that's not telling me anything," Buteo mumbled. "Just go and find him, you idiot!"

Somewhere else in the forest, Zaak was recovering from all the water he drank. He was coughing up water and fish. "Are you okay?" said Sheldon, as he patted Zaak on the back.

"Wow! Drinking all that water, really *LEAVES* you feeling pretty awful, huh? Get it—*LEAVES?*" Sheldon chucked. "Okay, bad joke. Seriously, how are you feeling?" Zaak yelled, "All washed up!" Then they both laughed so hard that they fell to their backs on the ground. Zaak asked Sheldon if he wanted to see something funny. Then he grabbed one of Sheldon's legs. "Hey, what's the big idea? Don't you even—" Sheldon cried. Before Sheldon could get out the last words, Zaak quickly spun him around on his back. "Ahhhh! This isn't funny!" Sheldon yelled as he went spinning around. Zaak laughed so hard that he wasn't paying attention to where he was going. He stepped right into the path of the spinning turtle. Zaak went flying through the air and landed headfirst into the ground. He pulled himself out of the hole just as Sheldon finished spinning. "That was fun!" Sheldon said breathing heavily.

"Wanna do it again?" Zaak said. "Thanks, but *NO THANKS*. I'm too old for this!" Sheldon quickly answered. "Okay, kid. It's time-out for fun. Let's get you in shape!"

Zaak and Sheldon were finding out quickly that Zaak had many abilities. He could shoot tree sap and small pieces of wood out of his fingers. He could camouflage himself to blend in with his surroundings (as long as he was in the woods). His body was protected by tree bark that acted as armor. He learned how to fly without crashing and how to manage his water-drinking habits. He could move as fast as a fish in water, but he could not move as fast on land. Zaak was shaping up to be well capable of protecting himself from Becky the Beaver. Sheldon warned Zaak that they had to be careful not to let Becky sneak up on them. So he taught him how to meditate and listen to the sounds of the forest around him. "Close your eyes and concentrate!" Sheldon yelled as he ruffled tree branches on the sides of Stick Boy's head. "Okay, kid, find me a squirrel!" Zaak concentrated and focused on the sound of a squirrel. Then he stretched out his arm, reached through the forest, and grabbed a squirrel. Then Zaak was told to grab a fox. So Zaak once again focused and reached through the woods and grabbed a fox. "Okay, kid, get me a beaver!" Sheldon yelled.

Zaak reached into the forest, and he pulled out a bear. "Beaver! Not bear, kid! We'll try again tomorrow." By then, it was getting dark, and Zaak started thinking again about his mother and father. "I wish one of my powers were to become normal again," he sighed. "That boy is in there somewhere, kid. You just have to believe it with all your heart," Sheldon said with comfort.

The next morning, Becky was still up to her evil deeds, terrorizing innocent creatures just for the laugh of it. "This forest is no match for Becky the Beaver!" she said as she snickered loudly. Meanwhile, her smelly sidekick, Buteo the Buzzard, hovered around surveying the area for a treelike creature. "I may as well be looking for a needle in a haystack!" Buteo uttered as he swooped down to take a closer look. He couldn't help but to notice a set of unusual footprints on the ground. He knew the footprints had to have come from an extremely large creature. Buteo landed and began to walk around observing the footprints. "It looks as if I have hit the old jackpot! I'll sit right here just in case this creature comes back through."

Zaak and Sheldon were walking through the woods, joking about how Becky's face looked when she attacked Zaak. "You can run, but you can't hide!" Zaak yelled as he crossed his eyes and stuck out his tongue. "More! More!" Sheldon yelled, shaking his head and moving his fingers as if he had razor-sharp claws. They both continued to laugh as they walked along. Zaak heard a sound coming from the bushes and stopped. "Shhh! I hear something," he said. They quietly moved forward, when all of a sudden, a pack of wolves jumped out in front of them. The wolves quickly surrounded them and started growling and clawing at them. "This is our territory. What are you doing here?" asked the pack leader. Sheldon answered, "We are just passing through. We mean no harm to you and your pack." "What, do you think we are stupid? Turn around and get off of our territory or be ripped into shreds!" the leader commanded. "Where is your little friend? She captured some of the pack, and we want them back!" Another wolf asked. "Are you talking about the beaver?" Sheldon responded. "She is no friend of mine! She's trying to eat me!" Zaak said. "Please, believe us.

We are harmless. In fact, we will help you find your friends," Sheldon said. The wolf leader told the others to stand down. "So who are you?" the leader asked. "I'm Zaak, and this is my friend Sheldon."

"I'm Alpha. This is my son, Saul, and my pack. The beaver has my daughter, Grace, along with a few others.

"Well, let's go get them," Sheldon commanded.

Becky the Beaver was still roaming through the forest, capturing animals. She had the animals in cages with wooden wheels on them and forced bears to pull them. She made a wooden vault and forced the animals to fill the vault with nuts and berries and wood. "Work, my little slaves, work!" she yelled. Just as she said that, she saw a little house. She sniffed the air, and it smelled as if something was cooking. "What is that horrible smell?" she said. "Let me go and see what's cooking."

She walked up to the house and looked in the window. She saw a woman in the kitchen, mixing something in pot. Becky thought to herself, *I could hang out here for a while. This is much better than my little house.* Becky formed a small twister with her tail and threw it at the horses' stable. When the wind hit the stable, it scared the horses. The woman ran out of the house to see what was making all the noise. When she saw that it was the horses, she ran down to the stables. "I knew my plan would work," Becky said. She went into the house and headed for the kitchen. When she got in to the kitchen, she looked into the pot. The food inside the pot did not smell good to Becky, so she poured it out. "How could you feed that to someone?" she said with anger. Then she tore through the kitchen, leaving every dish broken. She bit the sink and threw it out of the window with her mouth. Becky was on the rampage once again. She ripped the kitchen walls down with her razor-sharp claws. Then she went into the next room. There were pictures of a young boy all over. She picked up a card, and it read, "To Zaak and Idalene. Miss you very much, Dad."

"So this is where the stick boy lives. That means that this woman is his mother," she said. Becky knew that if she captured Zaak's mother, he would have to come and save her. Becky heard Zaak's mother come in, so she hid in the pantry. When Zaak's mother went into the kitchen, she saw the mess Becky made. "My goodness what happened in here?" she said. Then she started to clean up the mess. Becky thought this was her perfect time to capture her. She charged out of the pantry, cut up the kitchen table with her teeth, and quickly made a cage out of it. "Hello, Idalene!" Becky snarled. She clashed her teeth together and told Idalene to get into the cage. Idalene picked up the broom and tried to hit Becky with it, but Becky easily sliced it in half. "Get into the cage!" Becky commanded. Idalene started to run, when Becky said, "I have your son. Get in the cage, and I will take you to him." Zaak's mom had no idea that Becky was lying. She agreed to get in the cage and go with Becky. Once outside, she saw all the helpless animals in cages. She then dropped to her knees and cried. Becky laughed and said, "What's the matter, haven't you ever seen a dumb caged animal before?"

Becky had a plan. She would get Zaak close enough to hypnotize him with her hypnosight and force him to stand there as she tore him apart limb from limb. Every day she became more evil. She now had captured most of the forest animals, and she also had Zaak's mother. She would do anything to finally catch Zaak and cook him up in a wood stew. As they walked through the forest, Becky remembered Buteo. "Where is that stinky piece of rotten poultry? she screamed.

Buteo stayed there in the tree, waiting for the creature with the large footprints to return. He heard talking in the distance, so he hid himself in the tree and looked down. He was amazed to see that the description Becky gave was spot-on. Buteo was astonished and frightened at the same time. "I think we are on the right track," Zaak said. Just then, Buteo slipped on a branch. Immediately, Zaak grabbed him and used tree sap to shut his beak. "This must be one of the beaver's little spies. I can smell her scent all over him," Alpha said. The wolves wanted to demolish Buteo, but Alpha calmed them down. "Not yet," Alpha said.

Buteo began to flap his wings in fear. He did not want to be eaten by a pack of angry wolves. "Your leader captured some of our pack, and you are going to lead us to her," demanded Saul.

Meanwhile, Becky was still complaining about not hearing from Buteo. "That bird is useless! I could have found the stick myself by now. Man, I tell you, good help is too hard to find these days, isn't it?" she addressed the captured animals. The animals just shivered with fear. "Oh, you're not going to talk to me, are you?" she yelled. Just as they began to respond, Becky told them to shut up. Then she laughed loudly. Becky continued to laugh as she led the animals through the forest. She loved having slaves. "I'm the queen of the forest," she said as she held her head up high. Then she started to yell for Zaak. "I have your mommy!" she yelled. As she continued to yell, the wolves were picking up her scent. "She's close," Alpha whispered. Zaak camouflaged himself. All of a sudden, there were squirrels flying through the air. "We're being attacked by flying squirrels!" Sheldon screamed. "Take cover!" The squirrels did not affect Zaak, but the wolves kept being hit by them.

"There's too many of them! We have to move back!" Sheldon said. Then one of the squirrels knocked Buteo out of one of Zaak's hands, and he flew away. The squirrels were coming too fast for Sheldon and the wolves, so they ran back far enough to get out of dodge. They took cover behind some trees and discussed how to get past the flying squirrels.

Zaak was still where they first encountered the squirrels. He reached and grabbed one of them. He looked at it, and its eyes were dazed. He knew something had to be wrong with the poor creature. Zaak made his way around the flying squirrels. He wanted to see where they were coming from. As he went further, he heard laughing. "That sounds awfully familiar," he said to himself. Becky was laughing and calling his name. "Come out, come out, wherever you are!" she shrieked. "That's Becky!" he said. Zaak's heart began to pound. He was about to come face-to-face with his archenemy.

He moved further around the flying squirrels, and he saw her. "There she is," he said to himself. Becky had hundreds of little squirrels lined up, and she was swatting them with her tail one by one as fast as she could. Zaak knew he had to stop Becky from hurting any more animals. "That's enough, Becky," Zaak commanded. Becky stopped swatting the squirrels and sniffed the air. "That smells like my stick kabobs!" she said. "Show yourself! Are you too afraid to come out?" Becky asked. "Not anymore!" Zaak said as he stepped out so Becky could see him. "Boy, how you've grown. Tell me, when is the last time you saw your mother?" Becky asked Zaak. Zaak wondered what Becky was talking about. At that, Becky reached into one of the cages and pulled out Zaak's mother. "Does this face look familiar?" Becky yelled as she held Idalene in the air. Zaak had not seen his mother in two months. He had hoped his reunion with her would be better than this. He wondered what she would think if she found out that he was the creature that she ran away from at his house. Becky dangled Zaak's mother in the air as if she were a doll. "Put her down right now!" Zaak commanded.

"If you say so!" Becky snickered. Then she threw Idalene into a tree and cut the tree down with her razor-sharp claws. When the tree fell, it landed with the top of it hanging over the cliff. "Mom!" Zaak yelled. As he attempted to go after his mother, a gang of bears and deer that Becky hypnotized attacked him. The bears rushed at Zaak. Zaak knew that they were hypnotized. "You are no match for my bears of destruction!" Becky shrieked. The bears came at him from every direction. They were clawing and biting him while the deer charged at him antlers-first. The animals began to get the best of him because he did not want to hurt them. He had to find a way to stop them without them being injured. Zaak heard Sheldon's voice saying, "Concentrate, Kid, concentrate!" Then he remembered to listen to the sounds of the forest. He sunk his feet into the ground and focused. At that moment, he began to grow. He grew from fifteen feet to twenty feet, from twenty feet and taller. One of the deer charged into him, and water squirted out and hit the deer in the face.

The water hitting it released it from Becky's trance, and it ran off into the woods. Then Zaak knew exactly what to do. With his feet still in the ground, he sucked up all the water around him and started shooting water out of his fingers. Every time water hit one of the animals, it became normal and ran off safely into the forest. "You think you're so smart, don't you, you overgrown toothpick? I'll show you that I'm smarter!" Becky yelled. Meanwhile, Idalene managed to climb up into one of the tree limbs and sit down. *What's going on? Isn't that the same creature that I ran away from at my house?* she wondered.

Sheldon and the wolves had almost found their way to Zaak and Becky, when Alpha smelled the scent of the other wolves. He led the others in the direction of the wolves' scent. When they arrived, they saw all the caged animals. There were all sorts of animals in the wooden cages. Bears, deer, skunks, porcupines, rabbits, beavers, squirrels, snakes, and wolves were all trapped by Becky the Beaver. They could not believe that a little beaver could manage to capture this many animals.

44

They started releasing the creatures cage by cage. They did not know that Becky had all of them in a trance. "Look, it's Grace and the others!" Saul exclaimed happily. Grace and the other wolves were also hypnotized by Becky the Beaver. The animals started attacking them from every side. Sheldon was clear out of ideas. He, Alpha, and the wolf pack were outnumbered by all the animals. The deer were standing on their hind legs, boxing them with their front hooves. The skunks had them surrounded, with their tails pointed upward at them ready to spray, and the snakes hung from trees, striking downward at them. Sheldon and Alpha looked at each other. "If we let them, they will outfight us! We have to fight back. It's all or nothing!" Alpha said. Just then, Grace rushed at Alpha, and he jumped out of the way. Grace landed right into the river. "Hey. What's going on?" Grace said as she headed back to the shore. "It seems as if that psychotic beaver had you in some sort of trance," Saul told her.

Not too far away, Zaak and Becky were still throwing blows at each other. Zaak shot at Becky with his wooden finger darts, and she dodged all of them. Then he tried shooting her with water, and she just caught the water in her mouth and spat it out. "I told you, Toothpick, you are no match for me!" Becky snarled. "I thought you were my friend!" Zaak yelled.

"Friend? How can you be friends with your food?" Becky laughed. She chopped down a tree, and it fell right toward Zaak. Zaak caught it and laid it down. Then Becky quickly chopped down another tree, which landed on him and pinned him to the ground. Before he could get up, she dropped four more trees on top of him. Zaak could not move a bit. Becky began to swat Zaak in the face with her powerful tail. "What are you going to do now, toothpick? I've won!" Becky screamed with delight. Zaak squirted her in the face with water. Becky chopped down through the trees that were on top of Zaak to try to get to him, but her claws couldn't penetrate his bark armor. Then Zaak used his roots to grab Becky and wrapped her as tight as he could. Becky sawed through the roots with her razor-sharp teeth. Then the roots grew right back. Zaak mustered up all the strength he could and burst through the trees on top of him. He grabbed Becky by the neck, and she struggled to break free. While he was still holding her, Becky made a twister and threw it at the tree Zaak's mother was on. "Take that, Idalene!" Becky yelled as she hurled another twister. Zaak immediately let her down and rushed to his mother's aid. The twisters hit the tree and cut it in half.

The top of the tree fell off the cliff, with Zaak's mother still in it. As Idalene screamed for help, Zaak jumped off the cliff to save her. Becky stood at the edge of the cliff, hurling twisters down toward them. Zaak desperately attempted to grab his mother from the falling tree. *If I could just concentrate for one second, I can grab this tree,* he thought. Just as he grabbed it, the tree plunged into the river. Zaak went headfirst straight into the water. Becky looked over the cliff and laughed. "I told you that you were no match for me, Zaaky boy!" she screamed. Zaak's mother struggled to get to the surface while Zaak was still in the river. Zaak swallowed lots of water when he fell into the river. He was drowning. Idalene looked back and saw Zaak fighting to stay above water. She turned back, grabbed him, and pulled him to the shore. When they got to the shore, Zaak was coughing up water. He was very weak and could hardly move. Just then, Becky showed up. "What a lovely family reunion!" she said as she picked her teeth with her nails. "Too bad it has to end with Zaak being the dinner for the evening!"

Alpha and Sheldon were trying to fight off all the animals, when Buteo showed up. "Get back, you filthy bird!" Sheldon yelled as Buteo swooped down, clawing at their heads. The wolves jumped up to reach him, but he flew just out of their reach. "Ha-ha! You'll never beat Becky the Beaver!" Buteo squawked. At that moment, an eagle flew right into him. He fell down, and Saul grabbed him, but Buteo bit him and he let him go. Then Buteo flew away laughing loudly. The eagle that flew into him chased him, and they both flew out of sight. Looking at all the animals around them, it seemed as if there was no way out.

"I'm tired of playing games with you, Zaak!" Becky yelled. Zaak was still out of it. He was steadily coughing up water. Idalene patted him on the back. Becky lunged toward them and knocked her out of the way. Then she scratched Zaak on the leg. Her scratch penetrated his skin, and he screamed in agony. "The water must have weakened you." Becky said happily. "Now I finally have my chance to eat you!" Zaak tried to muster up all the strength he could to defend himself. Becky was clawing and biting Zaak everywhere.

Attempting to block her attacks, he waved his arms back and forth. As he waved his arms, leaves began to gather and twirl around. Becky was still attacking him as he moved his arms around faster. Soon the leaves were too much for Becky, so she had to stop. She tried to throw trees at him, but the trees were deflected by the force of the wind. The leaves were soon twirling around so fast that they began to catch on fire. Zaak's mother ran to safety behind a tree. Then Zaak began to get stronger. "Leave the forest or else!" he warned Becky. "Or else what?" she yelled stubbornly. Becky came at Zaak with all she had, but her attacks could not get past the leaves of fire. Then the leaves became fully engulfed in flames. Idalene ran up behind Zaak and touched him. When she did, the leaves turned into a golden fireball. Becky moved to try to bite him again, and he threw the fireball at her. When the fireball hit Becky, it carried her up toward the sky. As she went out of their sight she yelled, "I'll be back, Stick Boy! You'll see, I'll be back!"

As soon as the fireball hit Becky, the animals that surrounded Sheldon and the wolves were normal again and stopped attacking them. Then they ran to help Zaak.

The reaction from the fireball hitting Becky made it so bright that Zaak and Idalene could not see, and it became very quiet. "Zaak, Zaak, are you okay?" Idalene asked with concern. "I'm fine, Mom," he answered. "Where are you? Oh, there you are!" Idalene said as she walked toward the bottom of the cliff. "No, I'm over here," Zaak said. Then the bright light dimmed, and Idalene was standing by Zaak, but he wasn't moving. "Zaak! Zaak, wake up, honey!" she said as she shook his limp body. "Mom, I'm over here!" Zaak said again. When she turned, she saw Zaak, but he was back to normal. "How did this happen?" she asked him. "It's a long story," Zaak said as he walked over. Sheldon and the wolf pack arrived and saw Zaak standing with his mother. Sheldon knew immediately that it was Zaak. "Hey, kid, I see you got your wish! That's just wonderful!"

"So if everyone is all right, we are going home," Alpha said. "Thank you all for your help," Zaak said. "You know where we are if you need us. Wolf pack out!" said Saul as the wolves went back into the woods. "I knew you had it in you, kid," Sheldon told Zaak. "Thank you for believing in me, Sheldon," Zaak said with tears in his eyes. "Well, I guess I'll be on my way too," said Sheldon. They hugged, and Zaak said, "See you later, old friend." Zaak watched as Sheldon went into the woods. The stick man's body just lay there. It was not moving at all. Zaak picked it up, held its hand up, and said, "Limb, this is Mom. Mom, this is Limb." Idalene shook the stick man's hand as they both laughed and headed home. On the way back, Zaak found a piece of wood that was perfect for a head for Limb. "Now I find it," he said sarcastically. When they got home, Zaak went into his father's workshop and sat Limb on the table. "I'll work on you tomorrow," he told the stick man.

When Zaak got into the house, he asked his mother about Grandpa Mooty. "I haven't seen him since the day you disappeared. I thought you were together. I sure hope he's okay," said Idalene. "Me too," Zaak said. That night while in bed, Zaak thought of everything that happened over the past few weeks. He also thought of his father and Grandpa Mooty. The next morning, as soon as he got up, Zaak went straight to his father's woodshop. "All right, Limb. Let's attach that head!" he said with excitement. When he opened the door and looked, the stick man was gone!

Printed in the United States
By Bookmasters